P9-BYN-016

Patricia Polacco
Chicken Sunday

Philomel Books   New York

My special thanks to the Progressive Missionary Baptist Church of
Berkeley, California, without whose help and assistance this book could
not have been created. They furnished me with paper fans, hymnals,
and choir robes for research, plus a dear old yearbook with photos of
the Washington family—Stewart, Winston, and, of course, Miss Eula—
who so lovingly shared their lives with me when I was young.

Philomel Books, a division of The Putnam & Grosset Group,
200 Madison Avenue, New York, NY 10016.
Published simultaneously in Canada.
Printed in Hong Kong by South China Printing Co. (1988) Ltd.
The text is set in Stempel Schneidler Medium.
Book design by Nanette Stevenson.
Library of Congress Cataloging-in-Publication Data
Polacco, Patricia.   Chicken Sunday/by Patricia Polacco.   p.   cm.
Summary: To thank old Eula for her wonderful Sunday chicken dinners,
the children sell decorated eggs and buy her a beautiful Easter hat.
ISBN 0-399-22133-6 [1. Egg decoration—Fiction. 2. Easter—Fiction.
3. Friendship—Fiction.] I. Title. PZ7.P75186Ch   1992
[E]—dc20   91-16030CIP AC
10   9   8

To Stewart Grinnell Washington,
with love

Stewart and Winston were my neighbors. They were my brothers by a solemn ceremony we had performed in their backyard one summer. They weren't the same religion as I was. They were Baptists. Their gramma, Eula Mae Walker, was my gramma now. My babushka had died two summers before.

Sometimes my mother let me go to church on Sunday with them. How we loved to hear Miss Eula sing. She had a voice like slow thunder and sweet rain.

We'd walk to church and back. She'd take my hand as we crossed College Avenue. "Even though we've been churchin' up like decent folks ought to," she'd say, "I don't want you to step in front of one of those too fast cars. You'll be as flat as a hen's tongue." She squeezed my hand.

When we passed Mr. Kodinski's hat shop, Miss Eula would always stop and look in the window at the wonderful hats. Then she'd sigh and we'd walk on.

We called those Sundays "Chicken Sundays" because Miss Eula almost always fried chicken for dinner. There'd be collard greens with bacon, a big pot of hoppin' john, corn on the cob, and fried spoon bread.

One Sunday at the table we watched her paper fan flutter back and forth, pulling moist chicken-fried air along with it. She took a deep breath. Her skin glowed as she smiled. Then she told us something we already knew. "That Easter bonnet in Mr. Kodinski's window is the most beautiful I ever did see," she said thoughtfully.

The three of us exchanged looks. We wanted to get her that hat more than anything in the world.

Stewart reached into the hole in the trunk of our "wish tree" in the backyard. He pulled out a rusty Band-Aid tin. The three of us held our breath as we counted the money inside that we had been saving for weeks.

"If we are going to get that hat for Miss Eula in time for Easter, we are going to need a lot more than this," I announced.

"Maybe we should ask Mr. Kodinski if we could sweep up his shop or something to earn the rest of the money," Stewart said.

"I don't know," Winnie said fearfully. "He's such a strange old man. He never smiles at anyone. He always looks so mean!" We all agreed that it was worth a try anyway.

The next day we took a shortcut down the alley in back of the hat shop. Bigger boys were there. They were yelling. Eggs flew past us and pelted Mr. Kodinski's back door.

Just as the boys ran away the door flew open. Mr. Kodinski glared straight at us! "You there," he yelled. "Why do you kids do things like this?"

"It wasn't us," Stewart tried to say, but Mr. Kodinski wouldn't listen to us.

"All I want to do is live my life in peace. I'm calling your grandmother," he shouted as he wagged his finger in Stewart's face.

Miss Eula was waiting in her living room for us.

"Miss Eula, we didn't throw those eggs," I sobbed.

"Some big boys did," Stewart sputtered.

"What were you doing at the back of his shop in the first place?" she asked. We knew that we couldn't tell her the truth, so we just stood there and cried.

She looked at us for a long while. "Baby dears, I want to believe you. Heaven knows that I brought you children up to always tell the truth. If you say you didn't do it, then I believe you."

"It is too bad though," she went on to say. "That poor man has suffered so much in his life, he deserves more than eggs thrown at him. You know, he thinks *you* threw the eggs. You'll have to show him that you are good people. You'll have to change his mind somehow."

In my kitchen the next day we thought and thought.

"How can we win him over when he thinks that we threw those eggs?" Stewart asked.

"He doesn't even like us," Winston chirped.

"Eggs," I said quietly.

"Eggs?" Stewart asked.

"Eggs!" I screamed.

I went to the kitchen drawer and took out a lump of beeswax, a candle, a small funnel with a wooden handle, and some packets of yellow, red, and black dye.

Mom helped me show the boys how to decorate eggs the way my bubbie had taught us. The way they do it in the old country. We made designs on the egg shells with hot wax, then dyed them and finally melted the wax patterns off.

We put the eggs in a basket and, even though we were afraid, marched into Mr. Kodinski's shop and put them on the counter.

He raised his eyebrows and glowered at us. Then his eyes dropped to the basket.

"*Spaseeba,*" he said softly. That means "thank you" in Russian. "Pysanky eggs!" he said as he looked closely. "I haven't seen these since I left my homeland."

"We didn't throw those eggs at your door, Mr. Kodinski," we told him.

He looked at us for a minute. "Well, then, you have great courage to be here. Chutzpah, you have chutzpah!" Then his eyes glistened and his mouth curled into a warm smile. "Come, have some tea with me."

We spent the whole afternoon talking together, having poppy-seed cake and strong tea. He told us about his life. We told him about ours.

When we finally got the courage to ask about doing odd jobs to earn some extra money, he apologized and told us that there was no work. We didn't tell him what we wanted the money for. It didn't seem the right thing to do. Our hearts sank.

"I tell you this," he said thoughtfully. "These eggs are as beautiful as my hats."

Stewart, Winnie, and I looked at each other.

"It is almost Easter," he went on to say. "I'm sure that people would love these eggs. Set up a table and sell them right there in my shop!"

For the next few days we worked very hard. We made almost a dozen "Pysanky" eggs. When people came in, they picked them up and said things like, "Beautiful!" "Splendid!" "Intricate!" "Glorious!" We sold them all in one single day.

FOR SALE
real
UKRANIAM
EGGS

That afternoon when all the eggs were gone, we counted our money. We had more than enough for the hat.

Just as we were about to tell Mr. Kodinski that we wanted to buy the hat, he came out from the back room holding a beautiful hatbox…gift-wrapped! "Keep your money, children," he said softly. "I have seen Miss Eula admire this. It is for her, isn't it? Tell her that I know you are very good children, such good children!"

When Easter Sunday arrived, we thought our hearts would burst when we watched Miss Eula open the hatbox. She held us close, as big tears rolled down her cheeks.

Our hearts sang along with the choir that Sunday. She looked so beautiful in that hat. When it was time for her solo, we knew that she was singing just for us.

Her voice was like slow thunder and sweet rain.

Later that day as Miss Eula sat at the head of the table she said, "Oh baby dears, I can die happy now. And after I'm dead, on Chicken Sundays, I want you to boil up some chicken—bones, gravy, and all—and pour it over my grave. So late at night when I'm hungry, I can reach right out and have me some."

Then she rolled her head back and laughed from a deep, holy place inside.

Winston, Stewart, and I are grown up now. Our old neighborhood has changed some, yet it's still familiar, too. The freeway rumbles over the spot where Mr. Kodinski's shop once stood. I think of him often and his glorious hats.

We lost Miss Eula some time back, but every year we take some chicken soup up to Mountain View Cemetery and do just as she asked.

Sometimes, when we are especially quiet inside, we can hear singing. A voice that sounds like slow thunder and sweet rain.